WHEN WILL I READ?

Story by
Miriam Cohen

Pictures by
Lillian Hoban

Greenwillow Books

A Division of William Morrow & Company, Inc.

New York

Text copyright © 1977 by Miriam Cohen
Illustrations copyright © 1977 by Lillian Hoban
Printed in the United States of America

10   9   8   7   6   5   4   3   2

Library of Congress
Cataloging in Publication Data
Cohen, Miriam.
When will I read?
Summary: Impatient to begin reading,
a first-grader doesn't realize that
there is more to reading than books.
[1.   Reading—Fiction.   2.   School
stories]   I.   Hoban, Lillian.   II.   Title.
PZ7.C6628Wh   [E]   76-28320
ISBN 0-688-80073-4
ISBN 0-688-84073-6 lib. bdg.

To Dr. Jimmy Hymes,
Dr. Neith Headley,
Ruth Uhlmann,

and always
to Monroe

"When will I read?" Jim asked.
"Soon," the teacher said.

"But when?" said Jim.
"You know what the signs in
 our room say," the teacher said.

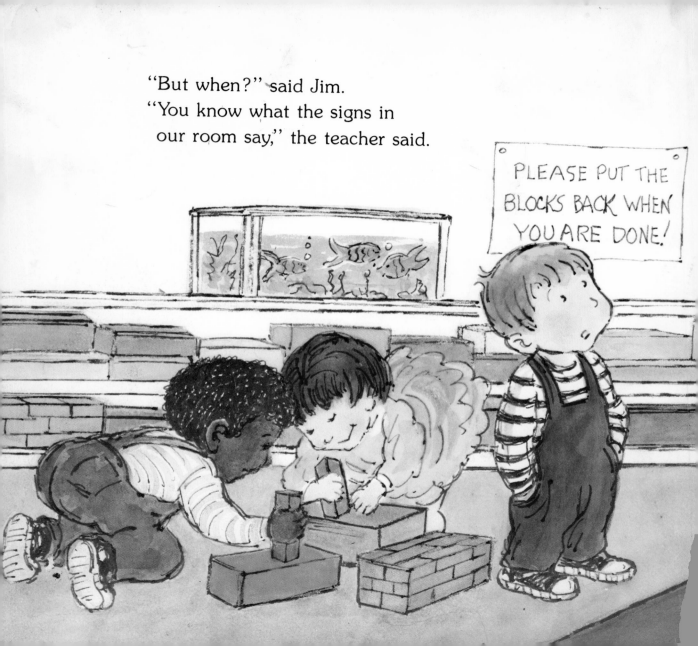

PLEASE PUT THE
BLOCKS BACK WHEN
YOU ARE DONE!

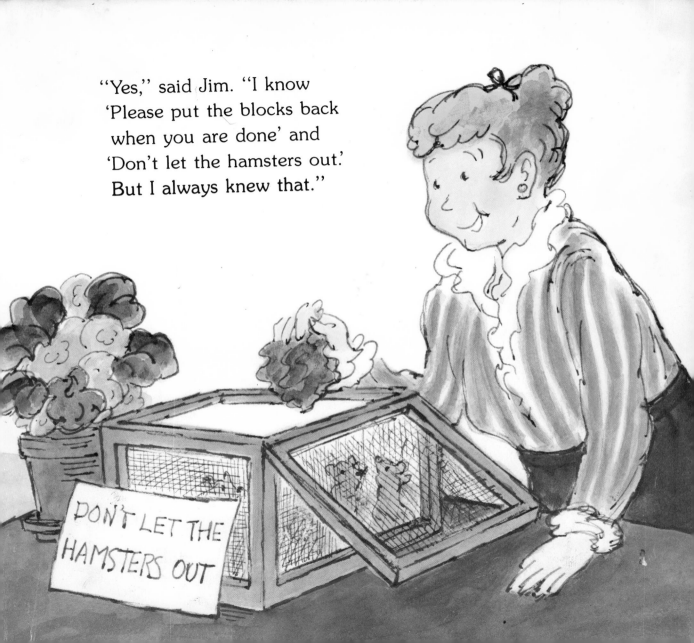

"Yes," said Jim. "I know
'Please put the blocks back
when you are done' and
'Don't let the hamsters out.'
But I always knew that."

DON'T LET THE
HAMSTERS OUT

"You can read your name," the teacher said.
"But that's not really reading," said Jim.
The teacher smiled. "It will happen," she said.
Then she went to get the snacks.

"I can read," George said.
"No, you can't," everybody shouted.
George took his favorite book
and told what it said under each picture.
"You only remembered it," Paul said.

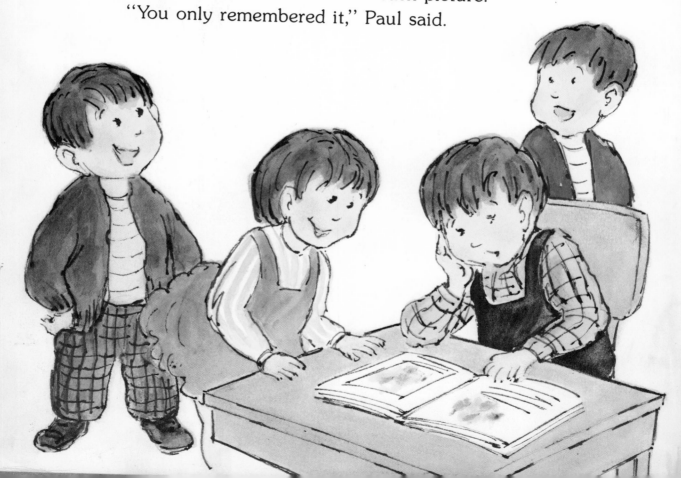

"That's how reading begins,"
said the teacher. "It begins that way."

Anna Maria was reading to her baby in the
doll corner. She could really read.
"Quiet," she said. "I'm reading to you."
But her baby would not be quiet.

Anna Maria said, "Oh, this is a bad baby.
He needs to be washed."
And she began to wash her baby
 very hard.

Jim said to Willy and Sammy, "Everywhere there is reading. There is reading about Smokey the Bear on the bus. There is reading on the Nutty O's box. Everywhere there is reading or writing, writing or reading."

Willy said, "On the Nutty O's
box it tells you to send for
a little airplane."
"Yes," said Sammy. "I did.
But it crashed right away."

Jim sat down at the table.
He put his head on his arms.
"Don't worry," the teacher said.
"There's no hurry.
You will read
when you are ready."

"But when will I be ready?"
Jim asked.
"You are getting ready
all the time," she said.

Just then there was a cranking, bashing,
clashing noise outside the first grade windows.
"Let's go and watch the garbage men work,"
said the teacher.
The class rushed out to the playground.

The garbage men lifted the big cans
and dumped them into the truck.
The crunching teeth ate up the trash.
One of the garbage men winked at Jim.
He said, "How are you doing, son?"

Then the garbage men
jumped on the truck
and drove away,
waving and smiling
at the first grade.

Afterward the teacher wrote
down everybody's story
about the garbage men.

Here is Jim's.

The garbage man is strong. He is not afraid of teeth that keep on eating the garbage. He just smiles and says: "How are you doing, son?"

Jim sat at the table, reading his story.
George and Willy and Sammy sat down with him.
Jim said, "I wish I could really read."
"A dog can read," Sammy said.
"No, he can't!" everybody shouted.

"Yes, a dog can," said Sammy. "He reads by the sniffs.
He sniffs and then he knows which dog came there before."
"But can a dog read the comics?" asked George.
Sammy and Willy fell down on the floor, laughing.

Jim was tired of worrying about reading.
He went to watch Danny and Paul and Margaret.
They were being firemen and their block city was on fire.
Danny yelled, "Bring the water over here!"
"No," said Margaret. "We have to save this man."
She and Paul began to put up a ladder.

"Hurry!" Danny yelled. "The fire is coming.
It will burn the hamsters."
He pretended to shoot water
on the hamsters' box.

Jim came to help Danny.
Then he saw that the sign
on the hamsters' box was torn.
It said, "Do let the hamsters out."

Jim ran to the teacher.
"Look!" he shouted.
"The sign says,
'Do let the hamsters out.'
They could get killed!"

"We can fix that!"
the teacher said.
And she began to
make a new sign.
Then she smiled at Jim.

"I told you it would happen,"
  she said. "You can read."
"I can?" Jim said.
"Yes," said the teacher.
 "That was reading.
  You really read the sign."

Jim and the teacher put the new sign
on the hamsters' cage.
"I waited all my life," said Jim.
"Now I can read."

DON'T LET THE
HAMSTERS
OUT!